jP
ZOL

Zolotow, Charlotte,
1915–

Summer is—

84 00620

# Summer Is...

Charlotte Zolotow

# Summer Is...

Pictures by Ruth Lercher Bornstein

Thomas Y. Crowell     New York

Text copyright © 1967 by Charlotte Zolotow
Illustrations copyright © 1983 by Ruth Lercher Bornstein
The text of *Summer Is...* was originally published
by Abelard-Schuman in 1967
Thomas Y. Crowell Junior Books, 10 East 53rd Street,
New York, N.Y. 10022. Published simultaneously in
Canada by Fitzhenry & Whiteside Limited, Toronto.

---

Library of Congress Cataloging in Publication Data

Zolotow, Charlotte, 1915–

    Summer is....

    Summary: Captures some of the joys and beauties of
each season.

    [1. Seasons—Fiction] I. Bornstein, Ruth, ill.
II Title.
PZ7.Z77Su 1983    [E]    82-45185
ISBN 0-690-04303-1    AACR2
ISBN 0-690-04304-X (lib. bdg.)

To Marty Symonds
—Charlotte

For my children,
Jesse, Noa, Adam, and Jonah
—R.L.B.

Summer is birds singing.

Summer is bare feet
and daisies and dandelions
and roses full on their stems.

Summer is porches
and cold lemonade
and dogs sleeping in the shade.

Summer is whirring lawn mowers
on still afternoons
and ice-cream cones
and watermelon.

Summer is long nights
and the stars low in the sky.

Fall is squirrels on the rooftops.
Fall is red and yellow leaves
and trees bending in the wind.
Fall is people holding their hats.

Fall is new pencil boxes
and dark coats
and heavy sweaters.

Fall is flocks of birds
flying like arrows in the sky.

Fall is chrysanthemums
and dry leaves and pumpkins
and cider and honey
and baskets of apples on roadside stands.

Winter is waking to the scrape of shovels.
Winter is snowsuits and heavy underwear.
Winter is sleds and ice skates
and wind.

Winter is snow
and pink skies early in the evening.
Winter is a white sun
and the moon before you're tired.

Winter is logs burning
and smoke from chimneys.
Winter is bare trees
lacing against the sky
and the smell of pines.

Winter is lamps lit early
and the warmth of home.

Spring is pussy willows
and yellow crocus pushing through
the melting snow.

Spring is cats prowling
and the green of new grass
and mud on your shoes
and warm rain.

Spring is the heavy sweetness
of hyacinth
and forsythia golden
along park and country roads.

Spring is worms in the damp earth
and growing things.

Spring is the hidden winter world
waking once again.